MOUNTAIN GORILLA

GORILLA MYSTERIES

BY MARY ELTING
Illustrated by
JOHN HAMBERGER

Platt & Munk, Publishers/New York
A Division of Grosset & Dunlap

 Printed in the United States of America. Library of Congress Catalog Number: 80-84449. ISBN: 0-448-47488-3.
Published simultaneously in Canada.

CONTENTS

ACKNOWLEDGMENTS

The author and the artist are indebted to many books and magazine articles for the stories and information in this book. For special help, the author thanks Franklin Folsom and Norma Morris. Paul Linger of the Denver Zoo and William Aragon, Curator of the Cheyenne Mountain Zoo, Colorado Springs, generously provided visits and time for questions about their gorilla families. Thanks also go to the Gorilla Foundation for recent information about Koko and Michael.

Mary Elting • John Hamberger

The Search for the Mysterious Man-Ape

"A terrible creature lives in the jungle. It looks like a man—but it never talks."

"Great hairy giants make war on African farmers!"

"Monsters kidnap people and carry them away."

Tales about the monsters frightened everyone who heard them for hundreds of years. But no scientist knew whether or not the stories were true.

"The evil-eyed animals tear people apart," Africans told European travelers. "Or they sit quietly in trees, waiting for a man to come along a path. Then they reach down and grab him and choke him to death."

Still, no one from Europe or America or Asia had ever seen one of these giants.

About one hundred and fifty years ago, a traveler did bring to the United States some huge skulls from West Africa. The scientist who studied them said they were not human skulls. They all had immense jaws and four great sharp fanglike teeth. Animals with jaws and teeth like that, he said, could certainly take terrible bites. Their faces, he added, must have looked so ferocious that it was impossible even to describe them.

There wasn't really much else the scientist could tell about these mysterious monsters just from their skulls. He had heard that a long time ago—many hundreds of years ago—an explorer from northern Africa had brought home three strange animal skins from West Africa. Writers who saw them said they looked as if they came from large manlike creatures. The explorer called them *gorillas*. But no one in modern times had seen the skins.

A few skulls and a few long-forgotten hides—that was all there was, except for the stories. What was a live gorilla really like? How fierce and strong could a gorilla be?

About a century ago, a young man from Philadelphia set out to solve the mystery. His name was Paul du Chaillu, and he loved adventure. So he journeyed to Africa to find a live gorilla.

There, near the equator, in the thickest of thick rain forests, Paul went exploring. But instead of just looking around for gorillas, he looked for a certain pear-shaped fruit that the Africans had told him gorillas loved. If he found it, he would probably find the animals nearby.

Paul struggled along through tangled vines and thorny bushes. He swatted strange insects that stung him and left painful sores. Sweat poured off him in the hot, damp forest, but he kept on searching for the pear-shaped fruit.

Before he found it, he came to a field of sugar cane. Many cane stalks were broken off and mashed, as if they had been chewed. Gorillas loved sugar cane as well as fruit, the Africans said.

Next, Paul saw huge footprints in the soil. They were much bigger than the prints of any human foot.

"Gorilla tracks," said the Africans.

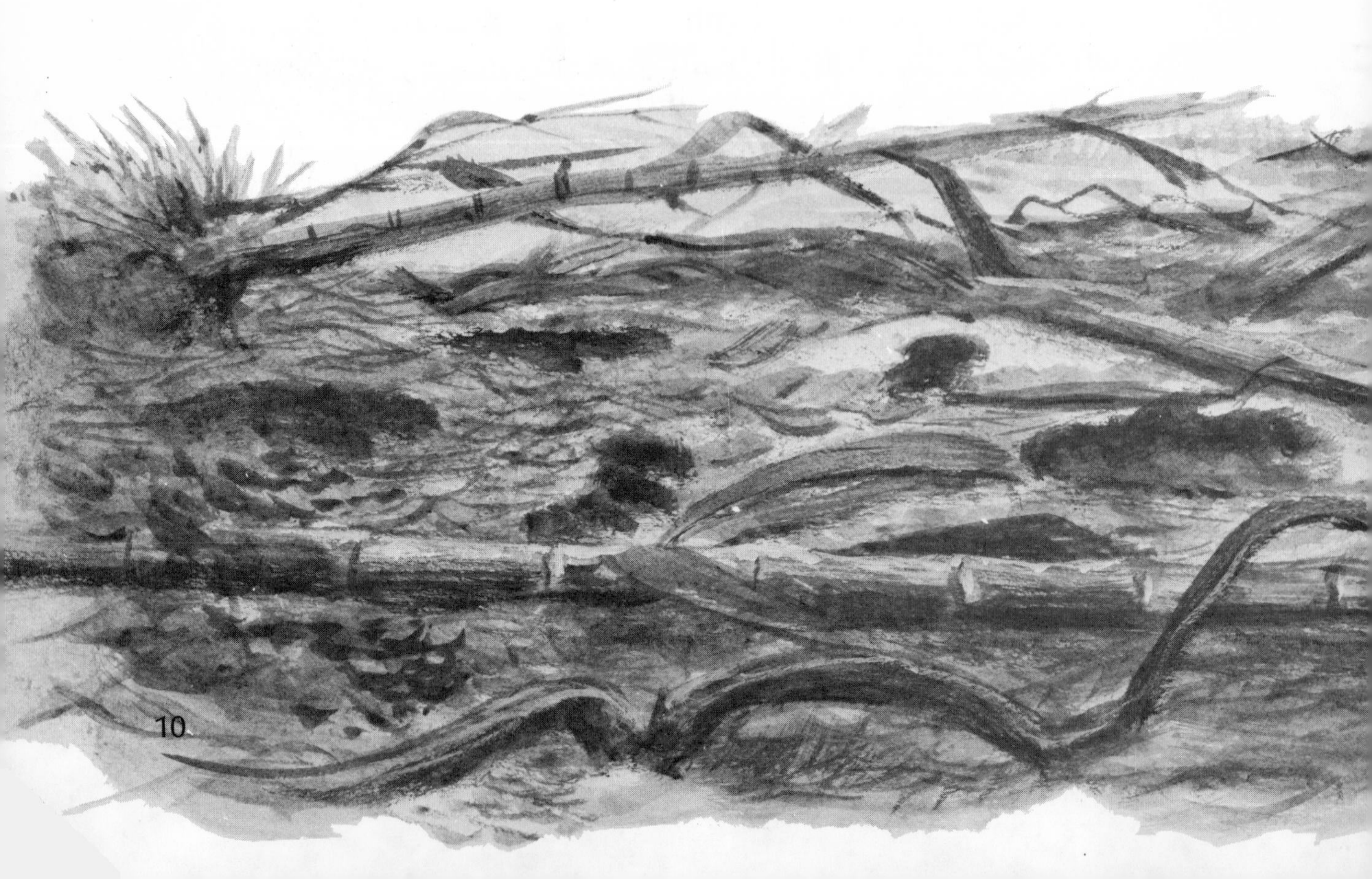

Then, across an open place in the forest, a great manlike animal appeared, half-hidden behind some leaves. At last, Paul was looking straight at the creature that no one from America or Europe had ever seen before—a live gorilla!

Paul had found what he'd been searching for. But the animal had also found Paul. It stood up and gave a fearful roar: "U-u-u-ah!" With its huge hands it pounded its chest—then ran straight at Paul.

For a moment the young explorer was too scared to move away. But he had a gun, and he fired it. The gorilla fell dead.

Paul stared at the animal he had brought down. It was huge—no doubt about that. Its chest was much bigger around than the chest of most human beings. Its arms stretched out much farther than human arms ever stretch. And the head was enormous. But when Paul measured the gorilla, he found it was no taller than a middle-sized man—only five feet six inches tall.

Paul du Chaillu had learned something about the mysterious animal, but he still knew very little. When he got home he did tell stories about gorillas that he had heard from other people. His tales were very exciting—especially the one about his narrow escape from the fierce, roaring beast.

Now there was more interest than ever in the gorilla monsters, the man-apes that lived in far-off jungles. Did they really make war on African farmers?

The farmers certainly warred on gorillas, Paul said. It often happened that a wandering troop of animals discovered a field of sugar cane or banana trees. They yanked up the cane and chewed the sweet, juicy stems. Instead of picking and eating the bananas, they ripped off the tough outside covering of the banana plants and devoured the soft insides. In just a little while a troop of gorillas could destroy a farmer's whole crop.

Of course, the farmers needed the food they grew to make a living. After their fields were raided, they would get together and start a gorilla hunt. It was a sad and bloody thing to watch. The farmers surrounded the troop and killed all of them with spears.

Paul told of hunts he had seen or heard about. Other explorers grew curious. They, too, went with farmers, and sometimes, if a mother gorilla was killed, they rescued her young one.

People who had zoos began to pay money for the little gorillas. What a fine exhibit the animals would make when they were grown-up and huge and fierce! But it didn't work out that way. One after another the young gorillas grew sick and died. Why?

Animal experts were puzzled. Perhaps if they knew more about what gorillas were really like, they could figure out how to keep them in captivity. One scientist who worked in a zoo made a trip to Africa. He had decided to watch gorillas in the forest. How did they behave? Were they really part man, part monster? Since he was afraid of them, he had a strong cage brought into the forest. Then he sat in safety in the cage and waited for a troop of gorillas to come along.

It was no use. Once or twice a lone animal approached. But the scientist had to go home with nothing except more stories that the farmers had told him about the ferocious man-apes.

Years went by. A few people who got baby gorillas raised them as pets or gave them to zoos. None of them lived to be very large or old. Now almost everyone forgot Paul du Chaillu, but they did remember the tales he and other travelers had told.

Solving the Monster Mystery

The Englishman and his guide stood hidden near a farmer's field in West Africa. Would a gorilla come to eat breakfast here today?

Before long, two huge hairy arms slowly pushed some branches aside. Parrots squawked and monkeys squealed in the trees overhead. But they didn't alarm the gorilla. The men held their breath as the big animal came out into the open. Suddenly he stood up on his hind legs, looked around, then began tearing a banana plant apart.

Now the Englishman almost laughed out loud. The gorilla sat down cross-legged and munched the juicy stem of the plant, just like a fat old man eating an apple.

The Englishman, whose name was Fred Merfield, wanted a better look. Unfortunately he made a slight noise when he tried to get his field glasses into position. The gorilla gave an angry cough and disappeared into the forest.

"Come on," Fred said. "Let's follow the Old Man."

That was not hard to do. Plants and small trees grew so close together in this part of the forest that gorillas made actual tunnels through the brush. The two men crept softly along the tunnel after the Old Man.

Fred knew they were getting close when he caught a whiff of gorilla smell. It was rather sweet and a little bit like burning rubber. He paused. Something dark filled the tunnel just ahead. It was the Old Man's legs!

The next instant the gorilla let loose a roar—the most awful sound Fred had ever heard. Before he could get out of the way, the Old Man leaped toward him and dashed past, giving him a smack on the hip with one enormous hand. The Old Man's sharp nails ripped through Fred's pants and left a long gash in the flesh underneath. But that was the only damage.

Farmers who heard the story were not surprised. If a gorilla was startled, they said, it would often lunge and strike a man. But a man who turned and ran away from a gorilla was in worse trouble. The animal would catch up with him and bite at his legs or bottom.

"Sometimes when a man comes home from a gorilla hunt, he can't sit down," a farmer said. "Then we laugh at him. The gorilla bit his behind because he was scared—and was running away."

In spite of his scratched hip, Fred wanted to know more about gorillas. Later he discovered a whole family of them in the forest. This time he took good care not to surprise them. While they were eating or napping, he stood still or sat motionless in a tree. Gradually, the gorillas got used to the man who kept quietly following them.

The Old Man in this family was very large, with a patch of silvery white hair on his back. There were some smaller, younger males in the group. But they and the females and the young ones all knew that the Old Man was their leader and boss. He always got what he wanted.

One day Fred was amazed to see a baby trying to grab a piece of fruit that the Old Man was eating. The big gorilla just kept the fruit out of its reach. At last the baby gave up. As it trotted off, the Old Man raised his hand and gave it a gentle, friendly pat on its bottom. Just such a hand, Fred thought, had torn a gash in his own human flesh.

Many other things puzzled Fred. Why did the big male leader sometimes rise to his feet, give a roar, and beat his chest with his hands? Holding the fingers cupped, he pounded—pok-pok-pok-pok-pok—so fast Fred could hardly count the blows. This might happen when another male, not a member of the family, came toward the group. The leader might dash at the stranger, running sideways, but suddenly stop and calm down. Why was the leader putting on such a show? Did he really mean to attack the newcomer? Why did he then stop acting so ferocious? And how ferocious was he, anyway?

More than twenty years went by before these questions were to be answered. In 1959, a scientist, George Schaller, came to Africa to study gorillas and to solve some of the puzzles. Gorillas, he knew, don't live everywhere in African forests. Their homes are mainly in two areas—around some volcanoes in the east, and in lower country near the ocean in the west. Those in the east, called mountain gorillas, are bigger than lowland gorillas. They have thicker, blacker, glossier hair. It was the lowland animals that Fred Merfield observed. George Schaller chose to study the ones that live on the slopes of the volcanoes. For two years he tracked and watched several groups of them.

There was an old story that mother gorillas and their children always built nests in trees at night. The male leader, people said, slept in a nest at the foot of the tree, protecting the family from harm. George found gorilla nests—plenty of them. He often located a group by following its trail from one place where it had slept to another where it had built fresh nests.

Sometimes, he found, mothers and babies did sleep in trees, sometimes on the ground. Big males usually built their nests on the ground. But once in a while they pulled vines together and made a kind of hammock. After the leader went to sleep, it was very hard to wake him until after sunrise the next morning. Did that mean he left his family unguarded against danger?

What *was* dangerous to gorillas? Almost nothing! Almost nothing except human beings, that is. George discovered that elephants never scared them or bothered them. Neither did sharp-horned buffalo. Leopards were supposed to be gorillas' enemies. But George saw one jump out of a tree close to a gorilla family. Nobody in the group paid it much attention, and it went away. Of course, the big cat might catch an old or sick gorilla, or a young one that strayed from its mother, but not the great strong males. Usually leopards went after easier game. The fact was that a leader didn't have to guard his group at night.

That was one puzzle solved.

Then why did some gorillas build nests in trees and some on the ground? The feathery tops of tall bamboos in the forest made soft, springy beds. Mothers and babies often nested high in the bamboos. But they were smaller than the big leader. His great weight would have broken the plants down before he got a bed made. So he slept where nest-building was easy.

Gorillas didn't spend a lot of time or care on their nests. They just pulled the tops of plants down around them and tucked some of the leaves or twigs underneath their backs. It didn't seem to matter whether the nest was cozy. George decided that gorillas simply did what was the least trouble.

Another puzzle solved.

Day after day, George followed one or another group. He almost never had to walk very far. When the leader woke up in the morning, he would yawn, sit up in his nest, and look around. Sometimes he saw a juicy plant growing nearby. Without leaving the nest, he would reach out, pull it, and have breakfast in bed. Often mothers with restless babies were already up. They and the older youngsters may have been nibbling plants that grew close to their nests. The forest was full of things they liked. In some places they found wild celery. In others, tender young bamboo shoots. They liked blackberries, and even blackberry leaves. Mothers picked the berries, carefully avoiding the thorns, and fed them to the babies. George discovered several dozen things that gorillas ate. Except for fruit and berries, the plants seemed to him very bitter.

After breakfast, the leader was ready to move on. He stood up and gave a special kind of grunt. Everyone else knew this was a signal. The youngsters stopped playing. Slowly the whole group went off behind the leader, nibbling as they walked.

The middle of the day was nap time—for everyone except the youngsters. Unless it was raining, the grown-up gorillas stretched out in the sun. The tiny babies curled up with their mothers. But their bigger brothers and sisters climbed trees, swung on vines, or slid down tree trunks. They wrestled or played a kind of follow-the-leader game. Sometimes they teased the adults. No one ever got angry with them. If they were too rough or annoying, the leader sometimes made a soft warning grunt. The teasing stopped instantly.

When the leader gave the signal, the group walked on again. Where there was something special to eat, they stopped. Or they might just grab bites along the way until it was time to make new nests and go to bed. Between morning and night they often traveled less than a mile.

George Schaller began to think gorillas were delightful and good-tempered animals. Once in a while some of the females would get into an argument and shriek at each other. But when the leader grunted at them, the quarrel ended. He seemed to be bossy but never mean. Was it possible that people were wrong about gorillas?

At last George concluded that gorillas were actually gentle, peaceful giants! Still, he had a lot of explaining to do. If they were not fierce and vicious, why did they have those terrible fangs? In all the times George watched them, he never saw them eat any other animals. Gorillas didn't use their fangs to tear up meat the way some other animals do. In fact, they were vegetarians. Their fangs helped them to tear away the tough outside parts of plants so they could get to the juicy, soft pulp inside.

Just the same, George had seen big males threatening people and other male gorillas. He had seen the bad scars from wounds that group leaders had given to farmers and hunters, and even to other males. He himself had seen and heard a huge male beating his chest while he roared and threatened. Was there something that people still hadn't noticed about this threatening performance?

George watched more carefully. When a leader was badly disturbed, he first grabbed a leaf and chewed it. Then he stood up and beat his chest and roared and thrashed the bushes with his arms. At last he charged. If there seemed to be no danger after all, he calmed down and went back to eating.

What do people do when they are upset? They may grab something to eat—just the way the gorilla leader did. If a person is really angry, he may let off steam by throwing things around or waving his arms and yelling—as the gorilla did. In real danger, a brave person fights—just as a gorilla does when hunters attack him or when he is threatened too much by another male.

George was sure now that he had the answer to one big question. Gorillas don't want to fight. They seldom fight among themselves, and they are so big they don't have to battle with other animals. The plain truth is—they just want to be left alone. The leader roars and makes threatening gestures partly to let off steam, partly to tell other animals—and people—to go away and tend to their own business. Most of the roaring and the ferocious threats are nothing but bluff!

The monster was not really a monster at all, and the mystery was solved at last. From then on scientists left their guns at home when they went to study gorillas in the forest.

Toto the Ape-Child

A very tiny, very frightened baby gorilla hugged Maria Hoyt and stopped screaming. The baby's majestic father had just been shot by hunters. They would send the great male gorilla's skin from Africa to New York. There it would be stuffed and shown in a museum.

The baby's mother and all the other members of her family had been caught in nets and clubbed to death. Only this nine-pound female baby remained alive. One of the hunters had captured her. Then he brought her out of the forest and handed her to Maria Hoyt.

Maria had never planned to adopt a gorilla. She and her husband were tourists in Africa. But the baby adopted Maria! So the Hoyts decided to keep her. Luckily they could afford to give the little gorilla a home and the care she might need. Soon the baby was given a name—Toto.

Maria had no idea how to raise a baby gorilla in captivity. She had to experiment as she learned about the little ape—which would not stay little very long. To begin with, Toto was so young she still needed mother's milk. Maria found an African woman who had milk to spare and who was willing to nurse Toto. Next, Maria found a young man named Abdullah who was willing to be a full-time baby-ape-sitter.

In a few weeks Toto seemed strong enough to travel. Maria and her husband set off with Toto and Abdullah to live in a hotel in Paris, France.

Paris is a long way from the hot African rain forest where Toto was born. She promptly caught pneumonia in the chilly city. But a whole team of doctors, with the help of an oxygen tent, managed to save her life.

While Toto was sick, she became used to a lot of loving care. When she recovered, she wouldn't go to sleep unless she was in bed with one of the Hoyts. She was getting spoiled, some French people said.

Toto grew fast—twice as fast as a human baby. She developed some strong likes and dislikes. She loved some of Maria's hats and patted them gently. She hated others. These she instantly ripped to pieces. She tore up some of Maria's dresses, too.

Wherever the Hoyts took Toto, she attracted a lot of attention. Finally, life in France became too complicated. So the Hoyts decided to move to Cuba. There the climate was warmer. Toto could have an almost tropical garden of her own to play in.

Getting to Cuba would not be simple. Gorillas were supposed to travel in cages on passenger ships that went there. But Maria was afraid Toto would die if she couldn't be with her adopted family on the voyage.

To solve the problem, Maria gave Toto some sleeping medicine, then covered her up with a blanket in a baby basket. Abdullah carried the basket onto the ship, just as if a human baby was asleep in it. From then on Maria kept moving Toto from one to another of the rooms that she and her husband and their servants used. When someone came to clean a room, Maria always had Toto somewhere else. Before the ship landed, Maria confessed to the captain, but the rest of the crew never found out what kind of baby was aboard.

In Cuba, in the city of Havana, the Hoyts and Toto and Abdullah lived in a big house with a very big garden. Around the garden was a wall, too high for Toto to climb. The garden walks were paved, and she soon found a special

use for the paving stones. She learned to draw on them. Some of her drawings even looked a little bit like the faces of human beings.

Toto learned other things, too. One day she discovered how to open and close an icebox. The cold, slippery ice delighted her. Every once in a while she stole chunks of it and hid them in the garden.

Abdullah, Toto's baby-sitter, finally had to return to his home in Africa. What would happen now? Would Toto let anyone else feed her and play with her? Maria Hoyt found a young Spanish man named Tomas who had taken care of chimpanzees, close relatives of gorillas. Tomas moved in with Toto—and stayed with her for more than thirty years!

In her own house in the garden, Toto now had her own special bed. At night it was closed up with bars, so she couldn't slip out and wander around and frighten people. Under her bed she had her own potty, which she learned how to use.

Tomas taught Toto to feed herself with a spoon and to eat whatever he ate. This was all right, except when Tomas had some food on his tray that Toto didn't have. She then helped herself to his dinner. At last, Tomas gave up trying to teach her good manners. He asked the cook always to put the same food on both their trays.

Toto liked to experiment in other ways. If a door was closed, she wanted to look on the other side of it. She

learned to turn knobs, and if a door was locked, she just broke the latch off. Then she found out about keys and what they were for. After that, she watched where keys were kept. When no one was looking, she stole them—and used them. That is, sometimes she did. Other times she lost patience and just smashed a door down. Once she sneaked out of a room when Tomas was inside. Then she quietly closed the door and bolted it shut. She had locked Tomas in, on purpose.

Toto had also learned to turn on water faucets. This worried Maria Hoyt. The water in Havana was not very pure. If Toto drank it, she might get sick. So all the faucets were changed. The new ones could only be turned on with a special key. That was one key Toto never was able to steal.

Toto loved games. One favorite was hide-and-seek. She would hide in the garden, then wait for people to find her. When they discovered her, she would scamper away and hide in a new place. This got to be a problem when time came for the game to stop. Since Toto understood what people said, the game could never end if the person who found her called out, "She's under the bench!" So her friends carried big sign cards. Of course Toto couldn't read. When she was located, a card would go up, telling where she was, and Tomas could sneak up and catch her so the game could be ended.

Gorillas have baby teeth, just the way human children have. When Toto's first baby tooth came loose, she went to Tomas and showed him how it wiggled. He tied a string to it and pulled it out. Then he put some brandy in Toto's mouth. The alcohol was supposed to keep infection from starting in the place where the tooth had been. Toto liked the brandy. She wanted more. Every time after that, when a tooth came loose, she got Tomas to pull it. And she always made very clear that she wanted some brandy.

Toto showed in many ways that she was much smarter than anyone thought a gorilla could be.

"Gorillas don't know how to use tools," some people said. But Toto could use a key to open a lock.

"Gorillas are stupid." But Toto certainly figured out quite a lot of things for herself.

"Gorillas don't have good memories." But what about this story? Toto developed a great friendship with Wally, one of the Hoyts' dogs. Together they romped around the garden and pretended to have fights. But one day some of the Hoyts' other dogs attacked Wally. A real fight started. Toto rushed to rescue her friend. She might have killed the other dogs if Tomas hadn't driven her into her house. In this kind of emergency he touched Toto with a special stick that gave her a mild electric shock.

Toto calmed down. A few days later she was out walking in the garden with Tomas when she sighted one of the dogs that had attacked her friend Wally. Angrily she started for the dog, and Tomas had to use his electric stick again. Obviously Toto had a very good memory.

One day she discovered a little kitten in the garden. From then on she carried it with her everywhere and cuddled it gently. Finally it grew up and had kittens of its own. Now Toto adopted one of the new kittens and began to lose interest in the mother cat. She even took the new pet with her when Maria had to send Toto away. The police in Havana had said that it would be against the law to keep a gorilla in the city any longer.

Toto's new home was a circus. Everyone hoped she would make friends with another circus gorilla named Gargantua. But Toto was now so used to people that she preferred Tomas. So he agreed to stay with her.

Every year Maria came for a long visit with her gorilla friend. In 1968, when Toto was about thirty-six years old, Maria thought she seemed rather tired. That day Toto died quietly in her sleep. She had lived longer than most gorillas live when they are free in the rain forest.

Maria Hoyt, who knew her adopted gorilla so well, thought that Toto was very much like a human being—except in two ways. Toto could not speak, and she lacked the human quality of self-control. When she didn't get her own way, she had tantrums. She used her immense strength to tear things apart when she was angry. She never figured out that it might be better to calm down than to yell and scream and throw things.

What Maria learned about Toto has helped scientists to go on and find out more about other gorillas. One thing they are discovering is that gorillas may be able to use words. These animals may be even smarter than Maria thought they were.

The Case of the Talking Fireworks-Child

"Flower stink!" Koko said that the first time she saw broccoli. Then she went on to make a rhyme. "Pink stink."

Once, when Koko had broken the toilet and wanted to avoid trouble, she said "Michael toilet!" She was blaming her playmate Michael. The fact is that Koko wasn't telling the truth—and she knew it.

The two young gorillas, Koko and Michael, didn't speak their words. But the people who took care of them understood what they said. Koko and Michael made signs with their hands, the way deaf-mute people do. They had learned the signs for words from Penny Patterson, a scientist at Stanford University in California.

Koko and Michael were not mute. They had voices. But the sounds of their voices were not the ones used in human speech. A gorilla's throat and tongue simply can't make such sounds. However, gorillas can easily make signs with their nimble hands. Koko and Michael learned to talk with Penny in sign language. They could even talk to each other using the signs they learned from her.

By the time Koko was seven years old she regularly used 375 sign-words. She used many others once in a while, and she has kept on learning more.

Koko listened while people around her were talking, and she understood a great many spoken words. That was how she learned to make rhymes in sign language. Besides "pink—stink," she made rhymes in signs for "squash—wash" and for "blue—do." If anyone said "candy" or "gum," she demanded some. She got to be such a pest that Penny had to do what human mothers sometimes do. She spelled out c-a-n-d-y and g-u-m, or other words she wanted to keep secret.

Once Koko heard two students talking about her. Was she a juvenile or an adolescent? Using sign language, she told them she was "gorilla." Another time Penny asked Koko, "Are you an animal or a person?" Instantly Koko answered: "Fine animal gorilla."

Koko's home is a trailer not far from Penny's house. In most ways she has led a very un-gorilla-like life after she was born in a San Francisco zoo on July 4, 1971. Because that was a day for fireworks, somebody called the new baby Hanabi-Ko. In Japanese that means Fireworks-Child. Soon everyone began calling her Koko, and the nickname stuck.

Penny first saw Koko when she was very small and very sick and needed care. Penny asked if she could look after the skinny little creature and teach her American Sign Language. And the director of the zoo agreed. Soon Penny moved Koko into the trailer, which became a combination home and nursery school.

Most scientists at that time still thought that gorillas were rather stupid animals. Teaching Koko wasn't easy, but Penny never doubted that her young student was intelligent. At first Koko sometimes nipped Penny during lessons. Or she refused to cooperate. Penny wasn't discouraged. Koko had to be smart in order to be such a brat, Penny said.

Gradually Koko learned to ask in sign language for what she wanted. Then she began to carry on conversations just for fun. She even helped clean the trailer. The most fun was scrubbing with a sponge—and tearing the sponge up afterward if no one was looking.

Like Toto, the gorilla who lived in Cuba, Koko loved to play hide-and-seek. She called it a "quiet chase." Unlike Toto, who had a regular bed and mattress, Koko had a sort of nest. She made it from some soft rugs and a motorcycle tire that Penny gave her to play with. Mattresses, Penny found, were too expensive. Koko liked to tear them up.

At rest-time Koko looked at the pictures in books. Sometimes Penny caught her making the sign for what she saw in the picture—"flower," for instance. Koko was talking to herself! She even tried to teach sign language to her dolls.

Penny was sure that all this proved that Koko was smart. But would a gorilla do well on an intelligence test? Penny gave her some IQ tests. Koko got almost as many correct answers as a normal human child her age. Remember that the test was invented for people, not gorillas. Good human answers to some questions are very different from good gorilla answers.

One day Penny introduced Koko to something new. She showed the gorilla a computer. The machine was something like a typewriter hooked up to a tape recorder. On some of the computer keys were signs that Koko recognized. When she punched a key, the recorder turned on, and Koko could hear a human voice pronouncing the same word that was on the key. She got the point right away. After that, she would punch the key with one hand, make the sign with the other hand, and a spoken word would come out. Koko was talking in two languages at once!

Still, there were scientists who thought Koko wasn't really using language. Only human beings, they said, could think and put thoughts together in sentences. But other scientists agreed with Penny. How could Koko make a rhyme or tell a lie if she wasn't thinking and using language? And Koko really did put words together into sentences, such as "me feel fine," and "time you quiet sleep." Also, Koko could make up her own words to describe things that were new to her. When she saw a mask, she called it an "eye hat." For a long-nosed Pinocchio doll she invented the name "elephant baby." That, Penny was sure, meant she was thinking.

Koko seemed able to make jokes, too. Once she called her flat nose, which had wide nostrils, a "fake mouth." When she was being mischievous, she often called Penny "nut" or "bird." But she could also invent insults when she was angry. Sometimes she made signs that called even her beloved Penny bad names.

Michael seems to be just as smart as Koko. He surprised everyone by answering questions about spoken sounds. When he was asked, "What word begins with *r*?" he answered with the sign for red.

"Can you tell me a word that begins with *s*?" Michael answered "sandwich" in sign language. "Can you tell me a word that starts with *b*?" "Bean, berry."

Michael can even make up stories. Once he told about a girl who got bitten by an alligator, so he hit the alligator and choked it.

Will Koko and Michael, or any other gorillas who learn to talk in this manner, teach sign language to their children, if they have any? Penny hopes they will some day. Then she and scientists everywhere can watch and find out whether gorillas will pass along the words they have learned, just as human parents teach language to their children. Scientists also want to know if people will be able to talk to gorillas who have learned hand-signs from other gorillas, instead of from human beings.

Many gorillas live in captivity, and babies are now born in zoos every year. Usually the keepers are allowed to give them names. There is even a kind of gorilla *Who's Who*—a book that lists all their names—such as Oscar, Roscoe, Tanga, and Frederika.

If all these gorillas learned to talk to each other in sign language, what do you think they would say about people?

More Puzzles, Solved and Unsolved

In the deep forest, on the side of an extinct volcano, lived a male gorilla who had a big patch of silvery hair on his back. He was leader of a group that had learned not to be afraid of a scientist, Dian Fossey. Dian called him Rafiki. That is an African word for "friend." She had spent hours and hours studying his group, and he was her favorite.

One day two human friends of Dian's visited this part of the forest. By mistake they came too close to Rafiki's group. Before they knew it, they were standing between him and a mother gorilla with a baby. The big silverback stood up, roared, and charged at the people. But he only touched one of them gently on the shoulder as he ran past. Dian's friend simply wanted to warn these human guests that they had better watch out.

After that, the two people took care not to disturb the group they were studying. They followed its trail through the forest until they came close. Then they got down and crawled along on hands and knees. That was almost the way the gorillas themselves usually walked. The difference was that a gorilla supports its weight on its feet and the knuckles of its hands.

Dian Fossey found that people standing upright are more likely to scare gorillas. Once, when she accidentally disturbed a group, five huge males came storming at her. She really was rather frightened. But she stood still, waved her arms, and yelled "Whoah!" All five stopped.

Usually Dian tried to behave as much like a gorilla as she could. She ran her fingers through her hair. She scratched herself and pretended to lick dirt off her arms. She chewed on leaves, though she hated the taste. And every once in a while she belched, just as her gorilla friends did.

Once Dian's human friends lay down near a group at rest-time. After a while a baby came over to get acquainted. He stood up and grinned and smacked his little chest with his hands. The next minute he climbed up on the woman's

back, knocked off her hat, and sat on her head. Bouncing and gurgling, he teased her—just as if she were his mother. Would the other gorillas worry about the baby? Perhaps the leader would think the woman meant some harm. There he came to investigate!

With one big hand the leader gently lifted the baby to the ground. After a calm, interested look at the woman, the huge fellow shooed the tiny one on down a path.

This baby was old enough to ride on his mother's back. When he was newborn, she always carried him held close in one arm, so she had to walk on two feet and the knuckles of just one hand. All gorilla mothers do this, and perhaps they find it tiresome. Anyway, as soon as the babies are a little bigger, their mothers often lay them on the ground while they rest. This really surprised scientists. No monkeys or chimpanzees or other apes ever put babies down. Why were gorilla mothers different?

The answer is that gorilla babies are different. When they are very young, their fingers don't grasp things firmly. A newborn chimpanzee holds tight to its mother's fur. It takes two people in a zoo to loosen a young chimpanzee's grip and get it away from its mother. A baby gorilla's fingers can be loosened easily. It doesn't resist when its mother lifts it in her hand and lays it down.

But doesn't this make life dangerous for the gorilla baby? Not really. Its mother travels from place to place on the ground. Monkeys and chimpanzees swing along from branch to branch through forest trees. Their babies must hang on or they will slip and fall and be hurt. Mother gorillas hold tiny babies tight. If older ones tumble off mothers' backs, they don't have far to fall. Sometimes a mother does climb into a tree to pick fruit or build a nest. Then she holds her baby with great care.

A little gorilla soon gets used to leaving its mother for a while. Sometimes the mother hands it to an older brother or sister to hold. Sometimes females, if they have no little ones of their own, do baby-sitting. When a youngster is about three years old, the leader may baby-sit. If its mother should die, the orphan is adopted by the leader. The big male sleeps with the little one and takes good care of it.

Each group of gorillas, scientists found, is somewhat like a family. Its members know and like each other. For the most part, they stay together. When males become fully grown, with silvery backs, some leave the group. If females from other groups join a wandering silverback, he becomes their leader, and a new group is formed.

As people followed gorillas through the forests, they began to notice a curious thing. One and all, big and little, the animals are afraid of water! They don't know how to swim. If their travels bring them to a stream, they make sure they can jump from one rock to another before they try to cross it. Or they look for a fallen tree to use as a bridge. The leader always crosses first.

No one knows why a gorilla won't try to swim. It certainly has enough strength. People have seen a large silverback pull up a small tree by the roots. They have watched a female, not nearly so big as a silverback, pull a weight too heavy for a grown man to pull. With electrical instruments

scientists have measured the strength in gorillas' arm muscles. Strong men's muscles couldn't match them. A circus gorilla named Gargantua used to play tug-of-war with people. He could pull harder on the rope than five men all pulling together.

Once in a while a silverback may start to tear things up and make a great mess—just for the fun of it. But mostly the leader and the whole group would rather do the same old things. They usually move along the same old paths around and around their part of the forest. They seldom eat new foods. Gorillas in eastern Africa love bamboo shoots, but those in western Africa won't touch them. Only the youngsters seem to be adventurous and full of curiosity about food. They will put anything into their mouths. If a baby finds something that tastes good, the mother may begin to eat it, too. But that's about the only change that happens among the peaceful, contented gorillas in the forest.

The Case of the Blue-Eyed Baby

White gorillas? Long ago a trader in Africa told an explorer that he had seen one in the distance.

Another time a guide whispered to a traveler, "Quick—a white ape!" But before the traveler could see it, the creature had vanished.

More than once an African farmer led an explorer to a dead gorilla that was supposed to be white. Always the animal turned out to be just old and gray. Every male gorilla gets a big patch of silvery hair on its back when it is fully grown. When it is old, its hair turns gray almost all over its body. Very old females also get many white hairs. These old graybacks were all that scientists found when they looked for white gorillas.

Then one day a farmer shot a gorilla who was raiding his banana grove. The dead animal, he saw, was a female with the usual black hair, black skin, and brown eyes. Clinging to her was a baby about two years old. And the baby was perfectly white!

The Africans called the little gorilla Nfumu, which means white. English-speaking people called him Snowflake. He was indeed just as rare as a snowflake would be in the rain forest where he was born.

Luckily, the farmer who found Nfumu knew the baby was valuable. He took it home, made it a nest in a cage, and gave it fruits and leaves to eat. Soon he was able to take the baby to a kind of half-way home. This was a special center where experts helped wild animals get used to captivity.

The red-dirt road to the center was dusty. When the farmer and the baby arrived, it was hard to tell that Nfumu really was white. Like all gorillas, he hated water, but he got a bath anyway. Afterward he cheered up and began to show a happy face. From then on he was probably the merriest of all the captives. Before long he was ready to move to the zoo in Barcelona, Spain. There, everyone called him Capito de Nieve; in English they called him Snowflake. Later he was also called "the vanilla gorilla"—because vanilla ice cream is white, of course.

Scientists studied Snowflake carefully. They gave him all kinds of tests, including intelligence tests. Snowflake was normal in every way and was just as bright as any gorilla that has the usual dark coloring. He was even smart enough to tell a fake gorilla from a real one. That happened when he saw a boy wearing a gorilla mask and pretending to be an ape. Snowflake snatched the mask off the boy's head. He knew a true gorilla when he saw one.

In one way Snowflake seemed to be a puzzle. Some people called him an albino. Like albino animals of other kinds, his hair had no color in it. His body looked pink because of the red blood showing through the pale skin. But his eyes were blue—like the eyes of fair-skinned human beings from northern Europe. Usually an albino has eyes that are pink.

Is there an explanation for the blue-eyed baby? Scientists now know part of the answer. They found that gorillas, like people, have cells in their bodies that produce a dark-colored substance called melanin. Those who have a lot of these cells have dark skin and eyes. Those with fewer of the cells have light skin and eyes. Some albinos have no melanin at all. That means their hair will be white and their skin and eyes pink, because the red blood is not hidden by melanin. But sometimes an albino has just a few cells that produce melanin. Snowflake had a few of these cells in his eyes, and that is what made them look blue.

Why do some people and some animals have a great many of the melanin cells while others have few or none? What makes them different? That is a mystery that scientists haven't solved entirely. They do know that differences in parents' bodies can be passed along to children.

Snowflake grew up and became the father of a baby gorilla. This new baby was black like its mother. Still, the people at the Barcelona Zoo hope that someday Snowflake may have a grandchild or a great-grandchild who will be another "vanilla gorilla."

Mini-Mysteries

The Stinging Nettle Case

Stinging nettle plants grow five or six feet tall in gorilla country. The stingers that cover the plants are little spikes filled with a kind of acid. When the spikes stick into a person's skin, they break, and the stinging stuff comes out. Walking through a field of these nettles, an explorer feels as if he is on fire.

Gorillas don't just walk through nettles. They eat them! Sometimes a gorilla breaks off a big nettle plant and peels the stem. The inside is crisp and juicy. Since the skin on gorilla hands is very tough, the spikes don't go through. But that's not the whole story. Gorillas often strip off nettle leaves and munch them, too. The lining of a gorilla's mouth is not as tough as its skin. Why don't the spikes on nettle leaves sting and hurt its mouth so much that it would leave them alone? The answer is still a mystery.

The Black Tooth Puzzle

A sleepy gorilla yawns. A big silverback opens his mouth to roar. The roar—and even the yawn—can be very startling if the gorilla's huge teeth are black. The strange thing is that zoo gorillas don't have black stains on their teeth. The only ones that do are those who live in the wild. Why? Do zoo gorillas brush their teeth? The answer is that they don't brush, although they might be better off if they did.

Dentists sometimes examine a gorilla in a zoo. They can do this if the animal has to have an anesthetic because it is

going to be operated on. While the anesthetic works, there is no danger in looking at its frightening teeth. What does a dentist find? Cavities, for one thing — the same kind that people have.

Gorillas living in the forest can get cavities, too. But what is to blame for their black teeth? That was what scientists asked each other at a meeting in 1980. Neither Dian Fossey nor anyone else present could answer the question. The best guess seemed to be that some chemical in the food that gorillas eat in the wild causes the black stain. It must be a chemical that is not in anything gorillas eat in zoos. But *what* it is still remains a mystery.

Is the Abominable Snowman a Kind of Gorilla?

People in the high mountains in Asia tell of a huge manlike creature called a Yeti or an Abominable Snowman. They say it is hairy, has enormous feet, and walks in a way that resembles a gorilla's walk. But no scientist has ever found a Yeti or even a Yeti skeleton. No photographer has ever brought back a picture of one. Some people have taken photographs of big strange marks in the snow that they think might be Yeti footprints. But something else could have made the marks. Scientists have found that the skins supposed to have come from Yetis really came from other animals.

In the United States, some people claim to have seen a large gorillalike creature called a Big Foot or a Sasquatch. But until someone can capture an actual Big Foot or a Yeti, there are only the stories to go on. People everywhere like to make up tales about terrible great beasts. In Africa there were stories about fierce gorillas. The gorillas turned out to be real, but they are gentle, not fierce—unless they are being threatened.

No one knows whether a Yeti or a Big Foot will ever be captured. You certainly can't catch an animal if it doesn't exist. Until we actually see one, we won't know whether or not it is like a gorilla.

Are There Any Pygmy Gorillas?

In Africa, near where gorillas live, there are some people called pygmies. They are normal in every way except that they are rather small.

Every once in a while scientists get reports that someone has found a pygmy gorilla. But when they have examined the skeletons of these "pygmies," they've been disappointed. Some were just young gorillas. Some were chimpanzees, which are smaller than gorillas.

Still, Africa has big stretches of forest where animals could live hidden from people. It has happened in the past that strange, unknown creatures turned up to surprise scientists. They did find a white gorilla, though they had almost given up hope. So there is still a chance that pygmy gorillas may exist.

The Case of the Ape's Appendix

People in the United States had heard about gorillas for 50 years. But until 1897 nobody had brought one across the Atlantic Ocean. That year a man who bought and sold animals in Europe got a baby gorilla. The place to sell it for a lot of money, he thought, was America, where it would be the first one ever exhibited.

ABOMINABLE SNOWMAN

The animal dealer set off across the cold North Atlantic Ocean in a ship, caring for the baby in his own room. But the little gorilla was used to warm weather and soon caught pneumonia. When the ship reached Boston, even the best doctors in the city could not save him. He died five days later.

At that time a great argument was going on. Many scientists believed that a very long time ago people and apes had the same ancestors. Not everybody agreed with this idea. Professor Burt Green Wilder wanted to see what he could find out. So he persuaded Cornell University, where he worked, to buy the dead baby gorilla. Perhaps if he examined its body he could tell whether apes and people are really relatives.

When Professor Wilder examined the gorilla's body, he discovered that it had an appendix. That is something that only people and apes have. Maybe an appendix was once useful to the ancestors of both apes and people. It no longer seems to serve any purpose, yet it is evidence that gorillas and people are indeed related. Professor Wilder's curiosity started the study of gorillas by scientists in this country.

The Case of the Sick Cousin

One day a gorilla in a zoo was very sick. The zoo keeper worried. So did the veterinarian, or animal doctor, at the zoo. The illness seemed to be one that people sometimes

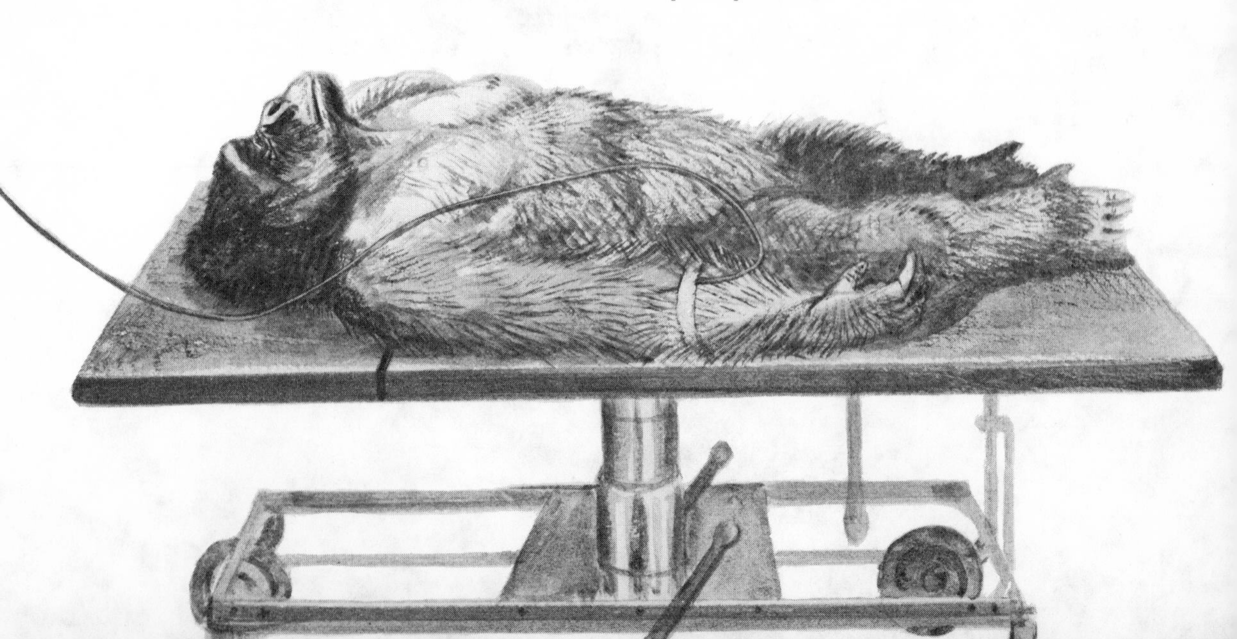

have. So the zoo keeper decided to send for a doctor who took care of people.

The doctor said the gorilla's blood had been harmed by sickness. The animal needed a tranfusion. That meant it might get well if they could transfer some healthy blood to its body.

Healthy people often give blood to help sick people. First, the doctor or a nurse uses a hollow needle to take some blood from a healthy person's arm. Then the healthy blood is allowed to drip slowly through a needle into a sick person's arm. The needle pricks a little when it goes into an arm, but the whole thing doesn't really hurt. Most people don't mind the uncomfortable feeling if they know their blood is going to help someone.

But just try to explain that to a big, strong gorilla!

There was no need to try, the doctor said. He would give the sick gorilla some medicine to make it sleep. Then he would take a few drops of its blood and test it to find out what type it was. Next, he would match it with the same type of blood from another gorilla, or if this were not possible, with human blood! Gorillas and people are such close relatives that this gorilla's life was actually saved by a transfusion of human blood.

And a gorilla can catch a cold, just the way you do. It can get pneumonia, a toothache, or arthritis that makes its joints ache the way human joints can ache. When a gorilla has a human disease, it is sometimes so sick that the zoo keeper sends it to a hospital for human beings.

Your body and a gorilla's body are alike in many ways. You have the same number of bones, and they are in the same places. Your hand and a gorilla's hand do not look exactly the same, but each has five fingers. Its feet have five toes. A gorilla's big toe sticks out more than yours does. It can grab things with its feet better than you can. It has arms much like human arms, only longer and stronger.

What about faces? You may think, after a quick visit to a zoo, that all gorillas look alike. But anyone who studies them can easily tell them apart. Each one has its own special look—just the way people have. Gorillas' faces show how they are feeling, too. They smile and frown. Gorillas bite their lips when they are nervous. When they are angry, they sometimes have tantrums, the way children do. They also get hiccups.

Young gorillas like to play, and they laugh when they are tickled. Children do, too, although they don't always like the way that tickling feels. Gorillas are a little different. They love to tickle each other and to be tickled.

They are also different from human beings in another way. Young gorillas in the wild almost never quarrel. But their mothers sometimes do!

Most of all, young gorillas like to be cuddled and loved. Even the great, powerful silverbacks are very gentle with the babies.

Like people, gorillas can be fearful and jealous and generous and curious. An explorer once followed a gorilla's tracks a long way into a cave. It had been exploring there, too—just out of curiosity. Sometimes, though, gorillas aren't the least bit curious. And that's just the way people sometimes are—or are not.

How does it happen that gorillas and people are so much alike? Scientists say that long, long ago gorillas and people had the same great, great, very-great grandparents. People and gorillas are actually cousins.

When scientists first began to study gorillas, almost everyone thought they were very stupid animals. Unlike people, they don't speak. They don't use sticks as tools the way chimpanzees do in the wild. But does that mean they aren't smart? The fact is that they get along very well in their natural homes. They don't really need to talk or use tools. They can pick all the food they need every day without saying a word to each other. All they need to get food is their hands and their teeth.

The more scientists learned about gorillas, the less stupid they thought the big apes were. They found that a gorilla has more brains than it needs to use in the wild. If Koko had grown up in the forest, we never would have known how smart she was. Her friend Penny Patterson gave her a chance to do things no one suspected a gorilla could do.

Do you think that sometimes happens to people?

The Case of the Bored Ape

How can gorillas be kept alive in captivity? For a long time no one knew the solution to that mystery. Gorillas usually died soon after they were put in cages. Why did such powerful animals just give up and fade away?

Gradually, zoo keepers have learned some of the answers. They found out, for instance, what kind of food is right for a gorilla. Here is what Snowflake had for dinner in the Barcelona Zoo when he was five years old: 2 pounds of bananas, 1 pound of apples, 1 pound of quince jelly, ½ pound of boiled ham, and ¼ pound of bread.

Sometimes Snowflake had chicken instead of ham. He also liked raw beef and yogurt and boiled eggs and rice and cookies. He was not a vegetarian as wild gorillas are. When meat came his way, he ate it, and it seemed to be good for him. Snowflake enjoyed almost any food—and lots of it. He had four meals a day!

In some zoos, gorillas eat a special manufactured food called monkey chow. It comes in hard little cakes like dog biscuits. Everything in it, including vitamins, helps to keep apes healthy. Because the bodies of people are so much like the bodies of apes, you could eat monkey chow, too. It tastes a little like rye crackers.

Gorillas in zoos have good diets now. But they need more than that to stay alive. Keepers have found that a gorilla may get sick and die when it is sad or lonely or bored. But what can they do to keep it happy? Perhaps the gorilla needs something to do—or friends for company.

In Chicago a famous gorilla named Bushman learned to play football. His keeper taught him to be an expert at tackling. He was also very good at carrying the ball. But he grew to be too strong. When he put a football under his arm and ran with it, he often squeezed it so hard that it broke. In one week, he squashed three footballs flat. That made the game too expensive, his keepers decided. They got him an old automobile tire to play with instead. He couldn't squash that—he just threw it around and had fun. Other keepers sometimes give their gorillas old tires. They can be toys during the day and nests at night.

Bushman loved to show off. He was always happy to have an audience watch him do tricks, and he liked people—usually. Once in a while a zoo visitor didn't please him for some reason. And then he would show off another skill. He could throw things with great accuracy. If the person he disliked came near his cage, he would hurl a boiled potato through the bars and hit his target—the "enemy's" head.

Activity kept Bushman from being bored. He lived to be 23 years old. Other gorillas in zoos have lived even longer.

Massa, who was then the oldest gorilla in captivity, had his fiftieth birthday in 1980. The Philadelphia Zoo gave him a party with a birthday cake and gifts. The cake was made of oranges, bananas, apples, a bitter green vegetable called kale, and a kind of cereal called Zoocake mixed with meat and vitamins. Best of all was the topping made of gumdrops, which Massa delicately picked off and ate one by one.

In Japan a keeper was sure the gorillas in his zoo would enjoy putting on a show. Most people had always said it wasn't possible to train gorillas to perform the way other animals did. At first this keeper had no luck. He tried to give the gorillas lessons in drum playing. But they suspected that the noisy, unfamiliar things might be dangerous. Then their trainer played a trick on them. He knew that they liked bananas. So he smeared bananas on drums. The animals couldn't resist. They licked the fruit off and got over their fear. Soon they learned how to beat out rhythms. Before long they could put on shows for visitors at the zoo.

Maybe you have visited a zoo where there is a thick window of glass or plastic between you and the gorillas. Why? The window is not there to protect you from the animals. It protects gorillas from you. The window keeps your germs from spreading to the animals. Behind the glass they breathe air that has been specially purified so they won't be so likely to get colds or pneumonia.

Sometimes a deep trench called a moat separates gorillas from people. The moat has steep, smooth sides, so the gorillas can't climb out and go exploring. But it usually does not have water in it. That is because gorillas can't swim. If they slip into water accidentally, they may drown, even in water that isn't very deep.

Many zoos now have areas with climbing bars or artificial trees made of cement. There, a whole troop of gorillas can play around and do stunts and keep from being bored. The

tree branches or bars aren't very high off the ground. Unlike chimpanzees, grown-up gorillas don't climb very high. They are too heavy.

There is sometimes a drinking fountain for gorillas to use. They like to turn the faucet on and watch it squirt. In the wild, scientists have seldom seen them taking a drink from a stream or pool. They may suck water from the fur on the back of a hand. But as a rule, the fresh green stuff they eat in the forest gives them all the moisture they need.

Nowadays zoo keepers try to have two or three or even more together in a big room or an outside area. It's not like family life in the wild, but the gorillas often get to like each other. Sometimes, though, a big silverback male does something he never does in the forest. He grabs a female's food—even if he has enough for himself. When that happens, the keeper may feed the female in another room. Or he may put the female's dinner outside some bars that are far enough apart for her hand to reach the food, but too close together for the big hand of the male to get through.

The first time a female gorilla had a baby in a zoo, newspapers all over the world had stories about it. But the mother didn't know how to take care of a newborn infant. There were no older gorilla mothers around to teach her what to do. This happened again and again in zoos. Either the babies died or the keepers had to find homes for the little gorillas where human beings acted as parents. Then they discovered a curious thing. By the time gorilla mothers had second babies in zoos, they often seemed to know what to do.

Mothers of second babies are almost always very gentle and loving. Usually a gorilla father likes a baby, too, and he may play with it when it is old enough.

The first gorilla to raise her baby in captivity was Achilla, who lived in the zoo in Basel, Switzerland. Her keeper called the baby Jambo, which means "good morning" in one of the African languages. Jambo was Achilla's second baby. When the first one came, she didn't know how to hold it so it could nurse. In order to feed that little one, the keeper had to take it away and give it milk from a bottle. But Achilla soon got the hang of nursing Jambo. She showed him off to other animals nearby and to the zoo director's wife, who was her special friend.

Every night Achilla slept with Jambo curled up in the automobile tire that was her nest. Finally, when he was two months old, she held him out and let her keeper hold him.

Zoo keepers are now so good at taking care of gorillas that there are babies whose own parents were born in zoos. A newborn gorilla is very tiny—much smaller than a human baby. But it grows quickly. Before long it is bigger than a human child of the same age.

If they aren't born there, how do gorillas get to the zoos?

Young ones sometimes arrive in the arms of a person who got them in the wild and who wants to sell them. (A gorilla costs a great deal of money.) Or the seller may bring a little one in a baby basket or a small cage. Big gorillas arrive in big, strong cages.

Once the zoo in San Diego, California, wanted a mate for one of its females. The Cheyenne Mountain Zoo in Colorado agreed to part with a huge silverback. But how would he travel? By truck or by train he would have to spend several days on the way. Even though he was so big and strong, he would be frightened and might get sick. Luckily, the San Diego baseball team heard about the problem. They had their own airplane for traveling around the country. Why not let the new gorilla come by air? So it was arranged. First his keeper gave him a pill to make him sleepy. Then his huge cage was put in the first-class section of the plane. And before he had time to be very upset, he reached his new home.

Before babies were born in the zoos, all zoo gorillas came from the forests of Africa. Most were babies or youngsters. At that time there were many more groups of them living in the wild than there are today. In one African national park it is against the law to kill mountain gorillas, but hunters often break the law. Some of these poachers kill them for food. Others shoot them just for fun. Farmers often to try to get rid of gorillas because they raid the farmers' fields and eat their food.

Scientists are afraid that before long there may be no gorillas left in the wild. Is it possible that the only way to save them is to keep them locked up in zoos? There they do have good care. Their babies are born there, and many of the babies live. Perhaps we shouldn't feel sorry for the gorillas that are locked up. We should be glad that zoos make it possible for these relatives of ours to keep on living on the earth.

The King Kong Case

When your grandparents were your age, they probably saw a movie about an ape-man monster called King Kong, who looked something like a gorilla. King Kong was much bigger than a gorilla is in real life—about fifty feet tall, so huge he could carry a beautiful young woman around in his hand.

The movie was so real that people could hardly believe King Kong wasn't a live gorilla. Actually, he was just a model made of rubber. And he was less than two feet tall! To show him in scenes with real people, photographers did a lot of tricks with their cameras. In some scenes they wanted to show how the frightened woman would look if she was actually held in a giant's hand. For these they used a big model of a hand and arm. It was eight feet long, and it worked like a puppet's hand. Cables moved the arm and closed the huge fingers around the live actress as she screamed and struggled.

Poor King Kong turned out to be a gentle, loving monster before he got killed at the end of the movie. By the time a new King Kong movie was made in 1976, almost everyone knew gorillas weren't monsters. Like George Schaller, they had learned that gorillas are really gentle, peaceful giants.

Index

LOWLAND GORILLA